MS Alice

Thank you for allowing me to come to your school & read to your students I had a wonderful time!

— Mike

Storyline concept by Mario Valbuena and David Alexander
Illustrations by Natalie Louis

Mario Valbuena
www.SaraSnapper.com

Printed in the United States of America

First Printing: July 2014
Sara Snapper

ISBN-978-1500264802

Sara Snapper
& the Magic Camera

mario valbuena
illustrated by natalie louis

AT THE BOTTOM OF THE OCEAN
WHERE THE SEA CREATURES DWELLED,
LIVED A COLORLESS
LITTLE SNAPPER NAMED SARA.

AND SHE LOVED ART.

SHE DREAMT OF NOTHING MORE
THAN TO BE COLORFUL
LIKE THE CLASSICAL PAINTINGS
SHE AND HER CLASS WOULD SOON GO SEE.

ON THE MORNING OF THE CLASS TRIP,
SARA COULDN'T WAIT TO SEE THE PAINTINGS
SHE HAD LEARNED SO MUCH ABOUT.

SHE WAS WAS ON HER WAY TO SCHOOL
WHEN ALL OF A SUDDEN.

SHE PICKED IT UP TO TAKE A CLOSER LOOK AND THOUGHT,
"THIS WOULD BE GREAT FOR MY CLASS TRIP."

BUT, WHEN SHE ARRIVED AT SCHOOL, THE SNICKERING SEAHORSES LAUGHED AT HER CAMERA.

THEY EVEN MADE FUN OF THE LUMP ON HER HEAD.

SARA DIDN'T CARE WHAT THOSE SILLY LITTLE SEAHORSES HAD TO SAY.
SHE SIMPLY GRABBED HER CAMERA AND FOLLOWED THE REST OF THE CLASS
AS THEY HEADED TO THEIR FIRST STOP IN SPAIN.
THERE, THEY WOULD SEE A FAMOUS PAINTING BY PICASSO.

'Las Meninas'
Pablo Picasso
1957

A GUIDE SOON EXPLAINED THAT THE COLORS WERE GONE BECAUSE NO ONE WAS COMING TO SEE THE ART.

Mr. Green

THIS MADE SARA VERY SAD.
SHE LOVED THE PAINTINGS AND
WISHED PEOPLE WOULD
COME SEE THEM AGAIN

IF ONLY SHE COULD HELP.

SARA DECIDED TO TAKE A PICTURE.
SHE WENT UP TO THE PAINTING,
SHE TOOK OUT HER CAMERA, AND...

THE COLORS CAME BACK!

SARA COULDN'T BELIEVE IT. THE PAINTING HAD COLOR AGAIN.
SHE DASHED OFF TO SHOW EVERYONE HER MAGIC CAMERA.

SHE SWAM
AS FAST AS SHE COULD.
"PROFESSOR SCALES,
PROFESSOR SCALES,"
SHE SHOUTED_

"NOT NOW, SARA,
WE MUST FIND OUT
IF THE OTHER PAINTINGS
ARE OKAY."

BUT, BEFORE SHE COULD SHOW ANYONE
THE COLORFUL PAINTINGS,
THEY HAD ALREADY LEFT TO THEIR NEXT STOP.

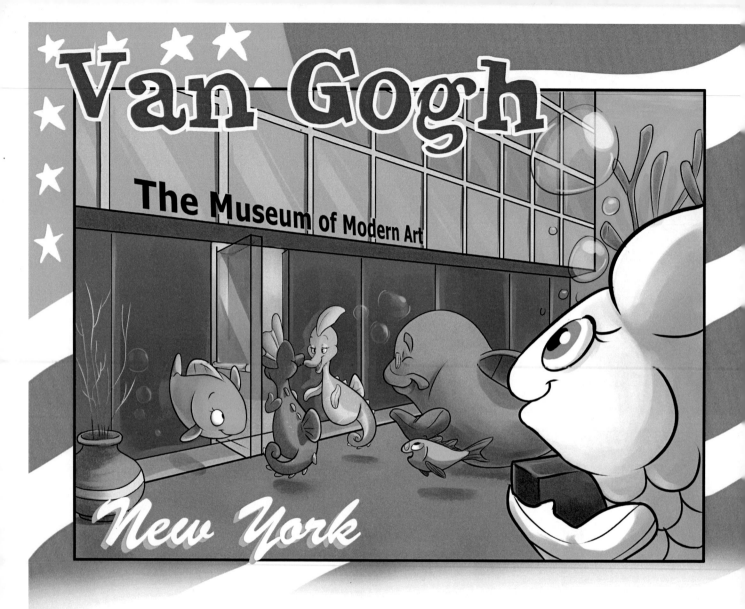

AT THE MUSEUM OF MODERN ART IN NEW YORK,
THEY PLANNED ON SEEING
"THE STARRY NIGHT,"
A FAMOUS PAINTING BY VAN GOGH.

BUT, JUST LIKE BEFORE THE COLORS WERE GONE!
SARA KNEW JUST WHAT TO DO.
SHE WENT UP TO THE PAINTING,
SHE TOOK OUT HER CAMERA AND...

THE COLORS CAME BACK!

BUT THERE WAS STILL NO ONE AROUND TO WITNESS THE MAGIC.
SHE DASHED OFF ONCE AGAIN.

"PROFESSOR SCALES,
PROFESSOR SCALES,"
SHE SHOUTED.
"NOT NOW, SARA, WE MUST
HURRY ALONG TO OUR FINAL DESTINATION."

PROFESSOR SCALES TOOK HIS CLASS TO THE LOUVRE IN PARIS
TO SEE HIS FAVORITE ARTWORK OF ALL TIME,
"THE MONA LISA."

BUT, WHEN HE SAW THE COLORS WERE GONE,
HE CRIED SALTY FISH TEARS NONSTOP.

"HOLY MACKEREL! I CAN'T BELIEVE IT. THE PAINTING HAS COLOR AGAIN,"
SHOUTED PROFESSOR SCALES.
"I TRIED TO TELL YOU," SAID SARA. "I TRIED TELLING YOU ALL!"

SARA SAVED THE DAY AND WAS A HERO.

SHE BROUGHT COLOR BACK INTO THE ART
AND JOY BACK INTO THE HEARTS
OF ALL THOSE WHO LOVED ART AS WELL.

JUST BEFORE HEADING HOME PROFESSOR SCALES
WANTED TO TAKE A CLASS PICTURE WITH SARA'S NEW CAMERA.

WITH A PRESS OF A BUTTON AND A FLICKERY FLASH,
SOMETHING MAGICAL HAPPENED AS HE TOOK THE SNAP...

Discover more online

www.sarasnapper.com

#KeepArtInYourHeart

 SaraSnapper    SaraSnapper   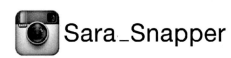 Sara_Snapper

Made in the USA
San Bernardino, CA
26 March 2016